Make-Believe Summer

A Victorian Idyll

MAKE-BELIEVE SUMMER

STORY BY
FRED CODY

ILLUSTRATIONS BY
ARTHUR BOYD HOUGHTON

A & W PUBLISHERS, INC.
NEW YORK

Published by
A & W Publishers, Inc.
95 Madison Avenue
New York, New York 10016

Library of Congress Cataloging in Publication Data

Cody, Fred.
　Make-believe summer.

　Drawings were originally published in
a book entitled Home thoughts and home scenes.

　SUMMARY: Text written to accompany 33 drawings
by a nineteenth-century English artist describes the
lives of a group of children and their summer on a farm
by the seaside in Victorian England.
　[1. Farm life—England—Fiction.　2. England—Fiction]
I. Houghton, Arthur Boyd, 1836–1875.　II. Title.
PZ4.C668Mak [PS3553.033]　813'.5'4 [Fic]　79-23067
ISBN 0-89479-058-7

For
Pat,
Martha,
Anthony,
Nora
and
Celia

PREFACE

This book could be described as an attempt, delayed by the passage of more than one-hundred years, to complete an artist's intention. The pictures of children, which are its chief feature, were first published in London in a parlor gift book called Home Thoughts and Home Scenes. The wood engravings that appeared in the original publication were created by a young English artist named Arthur Boyd Houghton (1836–1875). They were accompanied when first published by poems by Jean Ingelow and other women poets of the period.

How Houghton came to do the pictures is now a subject of conjecture. Though he struggled for recognition as a painter, Houghton supported himself and his family by working as an illustrator of books and periodicals. Always maintaining a standard of high quality, he produced hundreds of such illustrations. As part of his work, Houghton traveled widely to execute commissions for periodicals, the best known work of this kind being his series of engravings on life in the United States in 1870, appearing in The Graphic, a popular London illustrated weekly. These were among the engravings that were praised by Vincent van Gogh. Perhaps the most popular of his illustrations were for an edition of The Arabian Nights, *an assignment for which he was thought to be especially suited since he was born in India and lived there during the early part of his life.*

Speculation as to how Houghton's pictures for Home Thoughts *came to be created is almost irresistible. It is possible, of course, that the Dalziel Brothers, whose famous London workshop specialized in preparing engravings and illustrated books for the publishers of the time, may have commissioned Houghton to do the drawings. If so, he may well have quite calculatedly made a visit to a southern English farm, living for a time with friends in the country while working to complete his assignment. I am attracted to another possibility, however.*

All the biographical accounts of Houghton's life relate that he was blinded in his right eye in a childhood accident. It appears also that his vision in the other eye was subject to strain. To these handicaps—usually so discouraging to an artist—must be added the fact that Houghton suffered intensely from frequent attacks of migraine.

Undaunted, Houghton worked, it is said, in spurts of activity so as to take advantage of those periods when his sight was at its keenest. Often, when he did so, his eyes became irritated and inflamed. And no doubt the condition was worsened because of the artist's practice of drawing on the whitened surface of the woodblock, later made into a wood engraving at the Dalziel establishment. Perhaps these pictures were done during a period when he had fled his London studio for a recuperative stay in the country. In any event, a study of the pictures for Home Thoughts suggests that they were done while Houghton was a guest in a rural household.

These engravings of children form a unique record of a new chapter in the history of childhood among the industrialized countries. It is true, of course, that these are privileged children as there were relatively few parents in Victorian Britain affluent enough to allow their children such untrammeled freedom. Nevertheless, Houghton was perhaps one of the first artists to give us an intimate view of children, not as sweated factory workers or beggars on the streets, but as objects of affectionate indulgence.

The pictures are also notable for the way the artist has entered wholeheartedly into the world of childhood. The children are seen at play, but their activity is portrayed on their own terms; they are unselfconsciously absorbed in a realm apart. The pattern for such a separate state of childhood took form in the latter half of the nineteenth century, though only among families of means. It is the way, of course, that we are accustomed to seeing children in our own time.

Although the pictures have an appeal as a charming depiction of middle-class Victorian life, there are other—and possibly more compelling—reasons for their appearance a century later. Houghton was a remarkable artist and his work has value on the basis of its undoubted merit. His was a view of childhood that was not unclouded and, although his love of children is always evident, there is also present the "dark and mysterious" Goya-like quality in his work of which van Gogh wrote. The joy and vivacity of childhood are here, but so are the moments of introspective moodiness. Houghton, it may be noted, was the next to the youngest of four sons, his father a prosperous captain in the East India Company's Marine. His domestic scenes record a memory of what was apparently a happy childhood, but they reflect the shadows in his early life as well. It is these hints of the "other" side of childhood that impart to the pictures a curiously contemporary feeling.

Hence this book. The object has been to allow the pictures to tell the story of the children and their idyllic summer on an English farm. This, I believe, approaches the original aim of the artist; the matching of pictures and poems in their earlier appearance merely followed the publishing practice of the time. The engravings appear here with a modest and unobtrusive text close to the spirit and feeling of the present-day children's picture book. In this form, it is hoped the reader will now be encouraged to see in them the qualities of perceptiveness, sensitivity and originality, which make them an extraordinarily evocative view of childhood in their own time and in ours.

Of Houghton, himself, this should be added. As an artist associating with the pre-Raphaelite painters of his time, he was known for his ebullience and conviviality, a dashing Bohemian figure with a bushy beard and a jauntily worn black eyepatch. He was to find great happiness in his marriage with his lovely young Susan, but it was to end in three brief years with her death. In his late thirties, the artist turned increasingly to drink, apparently with the intention of bringing on his own death. He died at Hampstead of cirrhosis in his thirty-ninth year.

ACKNOWLEDGMENT

 owe a special debt of gratitude to
Paul Hogarth, a distinguished artist in his own right, who
has done so much in recent years to draw attention to the
artist whose work is featured here. Most of the biographical
details in the preface were found in Hogarth's book, Arthur
Boyd Houghton, Introduction and Check-List of the Artist's
Work, *published by the Victoria and Albert Museum in
London on the occasion of an exhibition there of Houghton's
work in 1975.*

ABOUT THIS BOOK...

ften, now that I am older and have children of my own, I take up the pictures you will see here and talk of the story they tell. And always they carry me back to a long-ago summer, which my sister Beth and I came to call our make-believe summer. I suppose I think of it in that way because it was a time between the end of one chapter in our lives and the beginning of another. It was a summer so full of wonder, of fear and strangeness, that it seems to have been not quite real—a kind of dream or fantasy.

You will want to know how we came to spend the summer in the great house near the sea. So I will tell you that Mother and Father had gone out from England to America just after they were married. He had been a farmer in England so they had made their way across the continent to the Great West to settle on a ranch in Montana. We had been born there and had come to love the house high on a mountainside where we had the feeling that we were a family working together in a world of our own. But then Father died and Mother was left with Beth and me and the new baby in the lonely house.

It was then that the letters began to come in a steady stream from Mother's family in England. Grandfather and Grandmother begged her to return. We heard the eager hope in her voice when she asked us if we thought we would be happy there. At last, we packed our few possessions and began the long journey across land and sea to England.

We knew that to Mother it was a homecoming to love and comfort. But it was not quite the same to Jennifer, Beth and me. For we were coming as strangers to a new land and a country house crowded with cousins, aunts and uncles. It seemed to us so different from the life we had known. We had so much to learn and understand.

Much of what we experienced that summer—the pain and, at last, the happiness—are in these pictures. And that is natural enough for they were drawn by an artist who grew closer to Mother—and to us—during the course of the summer. Just how that happened is part of our story, too.

Now I think we are ready to turn the page and begin the story of our Make-Believe Summer.

PART ONE
❧ *Settling In* ❧

It was Grandfather who welcomed us to the house. It seemed so grand and richly furnished. "You will be happy here, young ladies," he said.

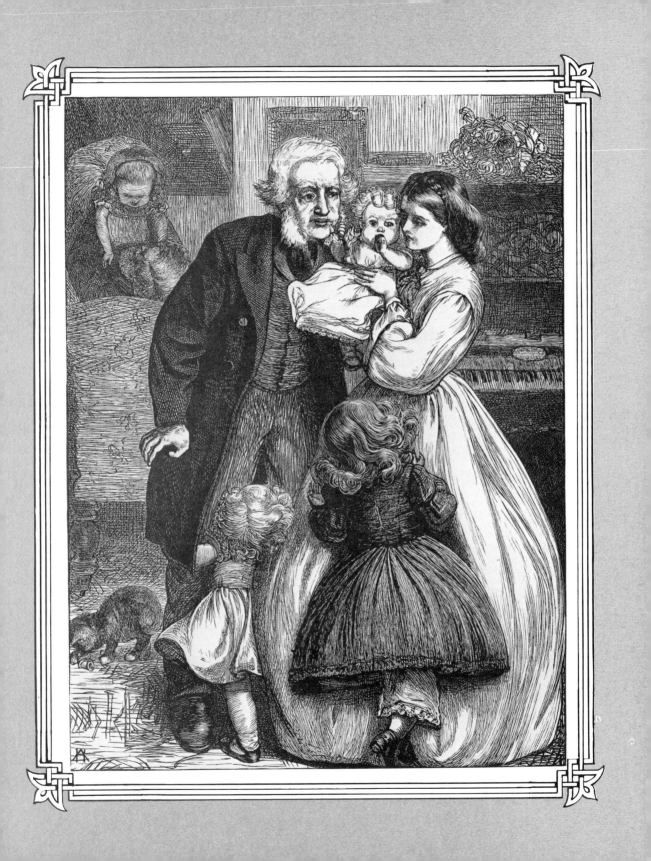

ext morning our cousins welcomed us! I finally rescued my doll from Tom's saw, but I didn't escape the spray from Peter's squirt gun.

It wasn't long before Beth and I were in the middle of a frightful rough and tumble.

But Tabby, the mischievous cat, soon became our friend and pet.

 **B**eth and I made certain we found moments when we could play apart from the rest in our old quiet way.

eth and I made certain we found moments when we could play apart from the rest in our old quiet way.

Playing train was something new for us—we had never had so many chairs.

*T*here were times, I must admit, when my thoughts turned back to those old days. But so much was happening, they seemed to grow fainter each day.

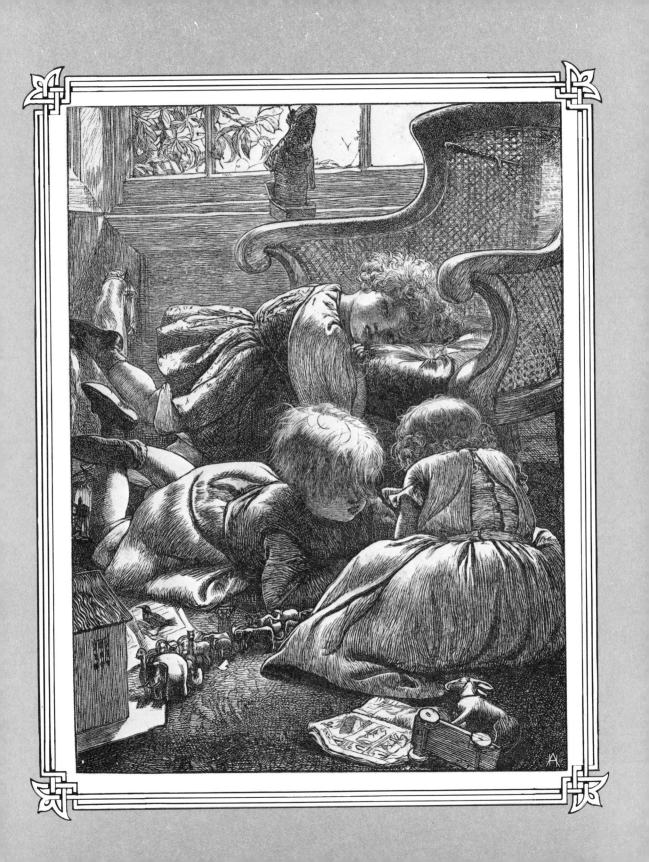

We certainly got into mischief sometimes. One day Beth put her whole fist into the jam jar. It was a struggle, but we finally helped her to pull it out. Mother had to be called to comfort her.

Beth had a terrible stomach-ache that evening from eating the jam. So the doctor came over, gave her some dreadful medicine, and she was sent to bed to get well.

other seemed happier every day. She and Jennifer often visited John, the artist, at his studio in a cottage close by.

 **I**n the late afternoons, during our "quiet times" just to ourselves, she told us of her growing fondness for him.

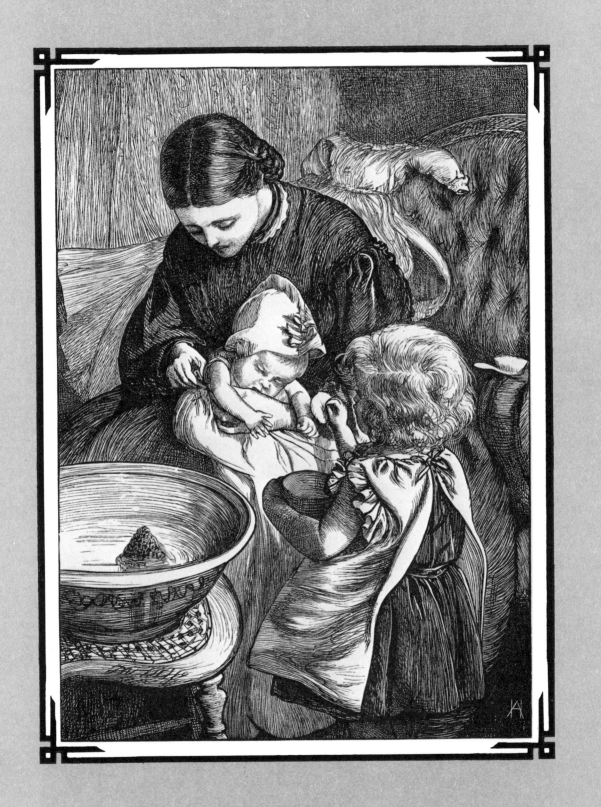

PART TWO
❧ *New Paths* ❧

s the days became
warmer, we trooped out into the fields and
woods. Bessie, who had a wooden leg, watched
us enviously. Later in the summer we grew to
be good friends.

PART TWO
❧ New Paths ❧

**A**s the days became warmer, we trooped out into the fields and woods. Bessie, who had a wooden leg, watched us enviously. Later in the summer we grew to be good friends.

 ow we loved taking Tabby and Tiger, the terrier, with us when we went out into the bright sunshine!

ovely wild flowers seemed to grow everywhere. Soon our cousins were helping us put some of them into pots to give to Mother.

I can't explain why, but I felt a kind of magic around an ancient oak tree in the forest. Everyone who came near it seemed to become a little odd, as though they were under a spell. And everywhere you looked there were faces peering through the trees.

To Beth and me the forest seemed enchanted. Once we came upon two beautiful ladies in flowing gowns tying pink ribbons on the lambs they had found there. "Oh, they must be princesses in a fairy story," Beth whispered. "Not very likely," said matter-of-fact Tom. "They're only some city folk visiting the Squire and having a lark in the woods."

The sunny fields where everyone worked at harvest-time were what Beth and I loved most.

I don't suppose Jennifer enjoyed it as much as we did. Anyway, we brought her out with us to the fields and took turns minding her during the long hot afternoons.

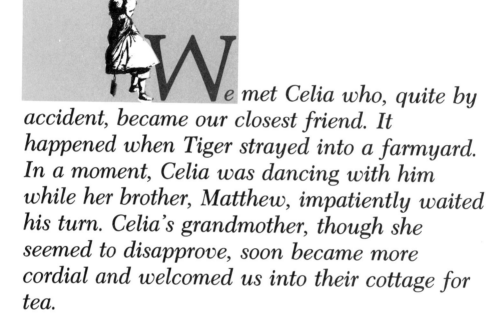 **W**e met Celia who, quite by accident, became our closest friend. It happened when Tiger strayed into a farmyard. In a moment, Celia was dancing with him while her brother, Matthew, impatiently waited his turn. Celia's grandmother, though she seemed to disapprove, soon became more cordial and welcomed us into their cottage for tea.

laying in the fields, we often saw Mother with John, the artist. How thoughtful they looked one day when Mother was plucking the petals from a daisy, saying "He loves me, he loves me not." We guessed that he cared for her when we heard him call her "my darling Emily."

PART THREE
A Sea-Change

Sea and shore were a completely new world to us. Our cousins laughed when we exclaimed in wonder at what was so familiar to them. When I think back on those days, I see now how John's pictures caught so much of what we were experiencing. He was seeing through our eyes, feeling as we felt. That was why he drew Jennifer trying to walk toward Celia and made certain he included the old sea captain who came by to romp with us each afternoon when he took his daily walk along the shore.

 first came to know John a little better one day when I had gone off alone to explore a grotto just after the tide had receded. I was terribly afraid a strange-looking creature at my feet was going to attack me. "Come this way, Meg," he said quietly. And I stepped forward to safety into his outstretched arms. I think that was when I first began to love him.

It took time, but I even came to like Joe, the cabin boy, home from a long voyage. He often came to play with Tiger. At first, I thought poor Tiger didn't like being covered with sand. But Joe meant no harm and Tiger really seemed indifferent. Meanwhile, Beth and I scrambled up and down the cliffs along the beach with the others.

There was almost too much excitement on the hottest day of the year when the beach swarmed with hundreds of people.

PART FOUR
❧ *Homecoming* ❧

**A**utumn was approaching now and sometimes fires were lighted to take away the evening chill. Then Mother sat with Jennifer nodding in her arms while she told us a story.

ven though it was the custom to play it only at Christmastime, Tom and Peter persuaded Grandfather to let us have a game of Snapdragon. So he brought a bowl full of brandy and Aunt Flo set it alight. Then we gathered around and plucked hot raisins from the flames. The darting hands set a hundred fantastic reflections dancing on the ceiling. What fun we had together that evening!

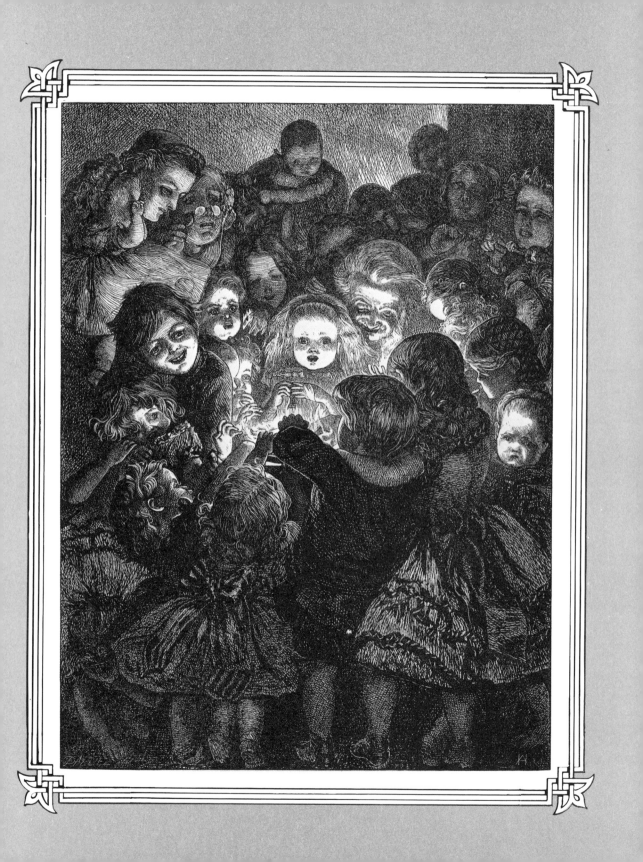

Tom and Peter seemed to be always prowling the house playing their pranks. And Cora, Peter's sister, was always their faithful companion.

**B**eth and I were always a little scared when we took our candle and went up the dark stairway to our room. Once we thought we saw a giant in a top hat. But it was only the shadow of the clothes on the hanger. Even so, I don't think we ever said our prayers faster before we jumped into bed and pulled the covers over our heads.

**O**ur love for Grandmother grew with every day that passed. We often came to her with our fears and worries for what she called a little "chin-wag." Beth still remembers sitting on her lap and listening to the cheerful, tinkling tune of the old music box.

olly Aunt Flo was also a favorite. She would set us to making funny clothes for Tiger while we sat with her, happy and at ease, in the sewing room. "As sure as I'm sitting here," she said smilingly one day, "you and Beth will soon have a very nice surprise."

*nd sure enough the moment came when I looked up at Mother's radiant face as she told me we were soon to be a family again. "And John," she said, "will be your Father as soon as we can be married. I know," she said, "you and Beth and Jennifer will come to love him as much as I do." We were to go to live in the cottage close to the great house, she told me. Then tears of happiness came to my eyes. For though I had grown fond of our cousins, I loved most of all the thought of a home of our own.*

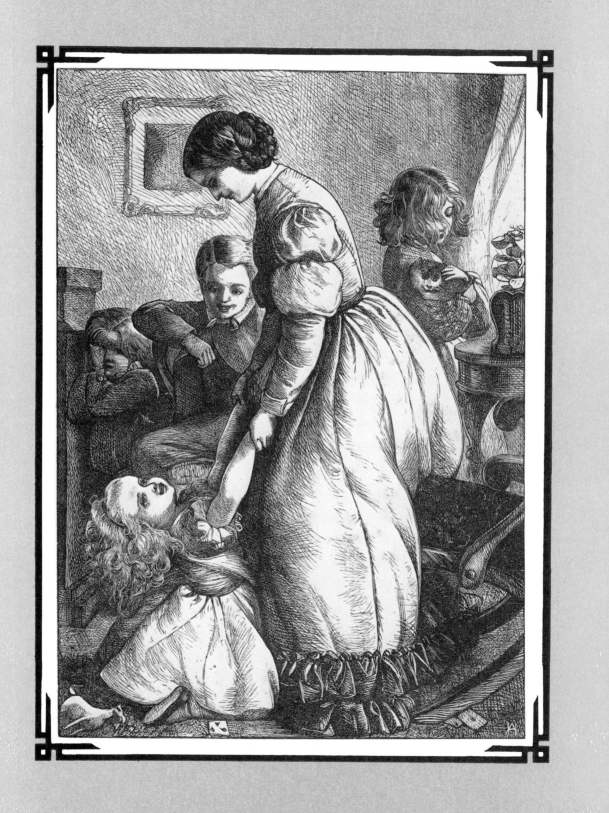

*ur weeks "in between" one life and the other were soon to end. We were to be a family again.*

So we come to the last picture of all. I always smile when I look at Father's drawing of the old farmer who never tired of staring at the Yankee children, and of Rufus, our pet raven, who often flew down to peck at crumbs around our feet. I suppose they might represent all that seemed difficult and strange about that first summer in England. Of the many pictures Father drew of us, this was the one we loved best. Our time of make-believe had passed. We were stepping forward now into the real happiness of our future life together.